Where's Woodstock?

Peanuts® characters created
and drawn by Charles M. Schulz

Text by Margo Lundell
Background illustrations
by Art and Kim Ellis

A GOLDEN BOOK • NEW YORK
Western Publishing Company, Inc., Racine, Wisconsin 53404

It was late summer—harvest time. Lucy had grown
nothing but potatoes in her garden, and everyone had
helped to dig them up. It was very hard work.

"The problem is mechanization," said Linus. "We
need a tractor, Lucy."

"A tractor!" Lucy said. "How in the world could we
ever get a tractor?"

"I don't know," Linus said. "But I absolutely refuse
to help with your garden next year unless we become
mechanized."

Snoopy watched as Woodstock delivered the last of
the crop and collapsed at the bottom of the heap of
potatoes. "Linus is right," Snoopy told Woodstock. "We
need a tractor."

After the harvest autumn came. The leaves turned
beautiful colors. Cold and rainy days arrived.
 Woodstock knew it was time for the Great Migration.
He had to fly south for the winter.

Snoopy knew Woodstock would return in the spring, but he was still sad to see his friend go. He gave Woodstock some money for the trip.

The Great Migration began. Woodstock and his pals headed off for warm weather.

Thanksgiving and Christmas came and went. Snoopy missed Woodstock even more during the holidays.

On Valentine's Day, Snoopy got a card from Woodstock. His little friend also sent a picture of himself, but it would still be many weeks before Woodstock returned.

Valentine's Day was a busy time for everyone. Lucy made a large, lacy card for Schroeder. She didn't care if he knew who sent it.

Peppermint Patty found a card in her mailbox. Even before she opened it, she knew it was from Pig Pen. It showed signs of his affection.

At last spring came. The air was warm and the days grew longer.

Snoopy caught spring fever. He danced among the daffodils. He thought about Woodstock. It wouldn't be too much longer before his little friend was back!

Everybody began to play outdoors again. Lucy oiled up her roller skates. She skated down a long smooth hill.

The soft sound of jump ropes turning was heard on every corner. Kids jumped and counted and took turns turning the ropes.

By the time the tulips bloomed, Woodstock still had not returned. But he sent Snoopy a letter, and he said he was bringing home a great surprise for everyone.

Woodstock enclosed a snapshot of himself typing the letter. Snoopy read the note very carefully. He couldn't wait until Woodstock came home!

More days passed, and still the little yellow bird did not appear. At last the World War I Flying Ace took it upon himself to search for his friend.

"Perhaps my friend has been shot down behind enemy lines!" he said. "Maybe he is being held prisoner!"

Finally the pilot spotted a familiar figure in the distance. Could it be Woodstock?

No! It was a small yellow bird, but it was Woodstock's friend Bill.

Snoopy was disappointed, but Bill had some important news. He said Woodstock wouldn't be home for many days. His trip back was going to be long and slow. Snoopy wondered why.

Even more days passed, and Woodstock did not
return. At last it was time to call the Foreign Legion.
The unit was put on Bird Alert. They searched high and
low for the little bird.

One courageous legionnaire walked for days from
oasis to oasis. Finally he saw a bit of yellow on the dusty
horizon.

It wasn't Woodstock. It was his friend Conrad.
Conrad said that he had traveled part of the way
back with Woodstock, but the trip was taking so long
that Conrad decided to come the rest of the way by
himself. Conrad showed Snoopy a picture he had taken
of Woodstock.

A few days later the World War I Flying Ace was about to go on another search when Linus came onto the airfield and stopped him.

"Do you realize that tomorrow is Easter?" Linus said. "That means the Easter Beagle will be coming."

The Flying Ace decided not to take off after all. "It won't be the same without Woodstock," he thought, "but you can't have Easter without the Easter Beagle!"

On Easter morning the Easter Beagle put on his show. The audience loved it.

Snoopy performed as well as he could, but he found his thoughts wandering to Woodstock. He tried his best to be a cheerful Easter Beagle, but he was worried about his little friend.

"It's no fun without Woodstock," he thought. "Why is he taking so long to get back?"

The next day Snoopy climbed up into Woodstock's tree. "Maybe he'll come back," Snoopy said, "if I sit here and wish very hard for him to arrive."

Lucy came by Woodstock's tree. "We have to start planting the garden today," she told Snoopy, "and you're helping!"

Snoopy couldn't believe his ears. Plant the garden? Woodstock always came back before Lucy planted her garden. It was his favorite thing to do. He wouldn't miss it for the world.

"Where in the world is that bird?" Snoopy said.

Snoopy went with Lucy to the garden. When they got there, Lucy began tilling the soil. It was hard work.

"We really need some farm machinery," Linus said. "This is too hard to do with these tools."

"Quit complaining and start working!" Lucy ordered.

Snoopy shook his head sadly. "I can see Woodstock now," he said, "digging the soil with his little shovel."

The next day Lucy brought a bigger shovel. The digging went a little faster, but it was still hard work. Late in the afternoon she went home, exhausted.

The next day she was back with her workers. In the middle of the afternoon they all paused when they heard the sound of a motor.

It was Woodstock! He had taken the money that
Snoopy had given him and bought a bird-sized tractor!
Everyone loved Woodstock's surprise. Snoopy was
overjoyed that his friend was back. The instant he saw
Woodstock, Snoopy made up a poem to celebrate his
return:

> "He's no impostor!
> He's no actor!
> Woodstock's back—
> Aboard a tractor!"

BEEP!

Snoopy felt better than he had in months. At last he could look forward to a fun summer. He might even offer to help Lucy with her garden.

"Gardening will be fun," Snoopy thought, "now that we have a little red tractor to do the hard work—and a little yellow bird to drive it!"